MARK'S DREAM TEAM

Mark is a City fan and his idol—striker Robbie Kidd—is presenting the trophy at the next five-a-side tournament. Mark's desperate to get Kidd's autograph and knows his team's got to win if he has any chance of meeting the top striker.

The only thing is, Mark's best friend Kenny is useless at football. But he can't leave him out of the side—can he?

Alan MacDonald was born in Watford. After university, Alan joined a travelling theatre company and acted in plays for schools all over Britain. He then trained as a drama teacher but decided to go back into theatre as a writer/director rather than teach. He went full-time as a writer in 1990. Alan now lives in Nottingham. He is a keen football fan having supported Watford FC from childhood and has described writing football stories as 'the next best thing to playing for England'. *Mark's Dream Team* is his seventh book for Oxford University Press.

MARK'S DREAM TEAM

OTHER OXFORD FICTION

MARK'S DREAM TEAM

Alan MacDonald

ILLUSTRATED BY
Clive Goodyer

OXFORD
UNIVERSITY PRESS

OXFORD
UNIVERSITY PRESS

Great Clarendon Street, Oxford OX2 6DP

Oxford University Press is a department of the University of Oxford.
It furthers the University's objective of excellence in research, scholarship,
and education by publishing worldwide in

Oxford New York
Auckland Bangkok Buenos Aires
Cape Town Chennai Dar es Salaam Delhi Hong Kong Istanbul
Karachi Kolkata Kuala Lumpur Madrid Melbourne Mexico City Mumbai
Nairobi São Paulo Shanghai Singapore Taipei Tokyo Toronto

With an associated company in Berlin

British Library Cataloguing in Publication Data available

ISBN 0 19 275217 0

1 3 5 7 9 10 8 6 4 2

Typeset by AFS Image Setters Ltd, Glasgow

Printed in Great Britain by
Cox & Wyman Ltd, Reading, Berkshire

Contents

The Last Autograph

The trouble with Kenny is that he's got too much imagination. Take football, for instance. Kenny imagines he's a brilliant footballer, he really does. To hear Kenny talk you'd think it's only a matter of time before he gets picked for England. Yet the truth is you wouldn't pick Kenny for your team unless everybody else had died of bubonic plague. It's not that he doesn't try hard, he does, it's just that he lacks basic things—like skill. Kenny's always telling me he's a midfielder, but that's only because he can't score goals and he couldn't tackle a flea. What he does most of the time is to run up and down the pitch, screaming 'Pass! Pass!' to anyone who will listen. And if you do pass, you won't see the ball again because he dribbles around in circles until he loses it.

Don't get me wrong, Kenny is my best friend and I'd stick up for him against anyone. But when it came to picking my team for the tournament I should have told him straight out he wasn't in it. That way I would have saved myself all the trouble that came later.

It all started with Robbie Kidd's autograph. You might think getting an autograph is a daft reason to enter a football tournament but that's why I did it. Robbie Kidd is City's five-million-pound striker and he's my all time favourite player. Last season he scored twenty-one goals for City. Almost every replica City shirt you see round our way has a number nine and the name 'KIDD' on the back. I've got one myself. That's why I was desperate to get his autograph to complete my collection.

I already had the autographs of every other player in City's first team. I got most of them at an open day at the City ground to meet the players; but somehow I never managed to get near Robbie Kidd that day. Whenever I looked there was a vast sea of people milling round him. I queued for ages but, just when I got near the front, Robbie announced he had to go. After that, getting Robbie Kidd's autograph became my personal mission in life. It was almost an obsession with me. In fact Kenny had taken to snoring every time I mentioned the subject.

Not long after, I had the chance to get Robbie Kidd's autograph. Kenny spotted him going into a hairdresser's and, once he'd convinced me he wasn't joking, we followed.

As soon as we walked through the door I knew we'd made a mistake. It was nothing like the barber's where I go to get my hair cut.

Everything about the place said '*expensive*' in big letters. Behind a desk sat a man with a ponytail who was staring at us as if we'd just brought in a nasty smell from the street.

'Can I help you?' he asked.

Kenny looked at me. His face plainly said, 'Run. Let's get out of here.'

But I wanted that autograph badly.

'Um . . . yes . . . ' I said hesitantly. Then, with a sudden inspiration, 'My friend needs a haircut.'

Kenny shot me a look of total horror. 'I don't think I do,' he muttered.

'Yes you *do*, Kenny,' I replied. 'Remember?'

Kenny glared back at me. Well, what else could I have said? My hair's short while Kenny's sticks up all over the place like a loo brush. It was obvious he was the one who needed a haircut.

A moment later we were sitting on one of the enormous sofas. I pretended to read a magazine, while scanning the room for Robbie Kidd.

'What are you playing at?' Kenny whispered furiously.

'Relax. Just playing for time,' I said. 'Look, he's over there.'

I'd spotted Robbie Kidd in the chair furthest from the door. He was leaning his head back over a sink having his hair washed by an assistant.

'Let's get this straight,' hissed Kenny. 'I am NOT having my hair cut.'

'OK, OK.'

'Have you seen the prices?'

I had. They started at twenty pounds and climbed steeply upwards. Twenty pounds—that was two months pocket money!

'As soon as I've got his autograph, we'll go,' I told Kenny.

'How?' he said. 'You told them I'm having my hair cut.'

I shrugged. 'We just say we changed our minds.'

'I'm going to get you for this,' muttered Kenny bitterly.

We waited. At last Robbie Kidd was having his hair dried with a towel. He must have made some joke because the girl drying his hair was laughing.

'Now!' whispered Kenny urgently. 'Get over there.'

But before I could move, a girl with short red hair came over to us.

'I'm Judy,' she said in a bored voice. 'Which one's for the chop then?'

'Pardon?' I said.

'Which of you wants his hair cut?'

I pointed dumbly at Kenny. Without a word he got up and followed Judy over to an empty black chair like a condemned man approaching the firing squad. All the time he kept looking back at me, imploring me to do something. He was about to have the most expensive haircut of his life. I felt in my pockets and quickly counted my change. It came to 75p—which I was saving for my bus fare home. It was all the money I had. Kenny must have had the same thought. As Judy picked up her scissors, he suddenly sprang out of the chair as if he'd been stung by a bee.

'I'm sorry, I've changed my mind,' he blurted out.

'What's the matter?' said Judy. But Kenny

didn't stick around for explanations. Before I could stop him, he'd bolted out of the door, slamming it so hard behind him that I half expected the glass to shatter. Everyone in the room abruptly stopped talking and looked over to see what the commotion was about. As I got awkwardly to my feet, they turned their gaze on me. 'Sorry about that,' I said. 'He's um . . . he's got nits.'

This got a bigger reaction than I'd expected. Several people gasped and recoiled from me in

horror, clearly believing I was crawling with bugs too. The ponytailed assistant flattened himself against the wall to let me get to the door. Out of the corner of my eye I could see Robbie Kidd watching all this and grinning hugely.

'He's having treatment but he gets embarrassed,' I burbled on. 'So, well, thanks anyway for the . . . um . . . '

At last I'd reached the door. I fumbled for the handle, got it open, and stumbled blindly out of the shop.

Outside, Kenny was waiting for me.

'Well? Did you get his autograph?' he asked.

I gave him a withering look. 'Thanks,' I said. 'You were a real help.'

The whole episode was a fiasco. Even now I cringe with embarrassment when I think about it. And it might have been the end of the story; there would have been no Endsley Eagles, no football tournament, and no autograph. But it didn't end there—a few weeks later I saw the report in the newspaper. It had to be Fate, I told myself. Fate stepped in to give me one last chance to get Robbie Kidd's autograph. Of course, at the time I hadn't a clue what I was letting myself in for—otherwise I might have told Fate to mind its own business.

Fate and Chips

I had just ordered five portions of fish and chips when we saw it. It was a Saturday evening and Kenny and I had been sent to the fish and chip shop to get supper for my family. The newspaper was lying open on the counter next to the plastic salt cellar and the vinegar pot. The page had got stains all over it from people's greasy fingers so I didn't take much notice. It was Kenny who spotted the picture. He stabbed a finger at a photograph near the top of the page. 'Look, it's Robbie Kidd.'

It was unmistakably him. What's more, there was an article underneath the photo which was even more interesting. It said:

CITY TO HOST SOCCER TOURNAMENT

Budding soccer stars will get a chance to show their skills next month in an exciting new tournament at the City ground. The competition is open to any five-a-side teams in the under-12 age group. City idol Robbie Kidd will be on hand to present the trophy to the winning side . . .

I didn't need to read any more. I was so excited I almost forgot to pay for our fish and chips. Checking that no one was looking I folded the page with the article and hid it in my pocket. Once we were outside the shop I said, 'Kenny, listen. This is it. This is the answer.' I read the article out loud to him.

'Good idea, we could go along and watch,' he said.

I shook my head. He hadn't grasped it yet. 'This is how I'll meet Robbie Kidd,' I said. 'I'll be standing right next to him.'

'How do you work that out?'

'When he hands me the trophy, thicko. I'm

going to enter a team in that tournament and win.'

Kenny gaped at me as he took this in. Then his face lit up.

'Yeah,' he said. 'We could as well. We could get Martin—he's the best goalie in the whole school. And Rashid—he'd play . . . '

'I'll play up front,' I said.

'And I'll be midfield . . . ' said Kenny.

I stopped in my tracks. 'You?'

'Yeah, of course,' said Kenny. 'Midfield. I always play midfield.' He blinked at me for a moment and adjusted his glasses.

'Right,' I agreed quickly. 'You in midfield and me up front. We're bound to win. We'll be unstoppable.'

All the way home and over supper, Kenny and I talked excitedly about the tournament. We discussed our team colours and what we should call ourselves. But all the time there was a nagging doubt at the back of my mind. It was Kenny. OK, I'm not saying I'm wonder boy myself but I'm good enough to make the subs' bench for our school team. But Kenny? As

I've mentioned he's as much use as a short-sighted penguin. You can imagine how thrilled I felt having him on my team. I wanted to win that tournament more than anything. Robbie Kidd would be there watching and I pictured myself coming away with the trophy under my arm and his autograph in my book. But my plan all depended on winning. If we were knocked out before the final I might never get anywhere near Robbie Kidd. Kenny was the weak link in the whole plan. With him on our side I didn't see us getting past the first round.

That was my mistake. I should have told him there and then. But I just couldn't do it. When I looked at Kenny, I knew how much it would hurt his feelings if I left him out. Besides, he was my best friend and we did everything together. So I said nothing and let him go on believing he'd be in the team. Stupid, I know, but I was only just getting started. You'd be surprised just how stupid I can be.

Kenny and I sat down right away and completed the entry form at the bottom of the newspaper article. We called our team Endsley

Eagles (after Endsley Drive, which is the name of my road.) Kenny wanted to call us Haddock United so that we could get sponsorship from the fish and chip shop, but I said no one would take us seriously with a name like that. Sealing the envelope, I placed it on the table ready to post in the morning.

As I said goodbye to Kenny that evening, he was so excited he could hardly stop talking.

'Wait till they hear this at school,' he kept saying. 'Me! Playing at the City ground. Think of that, eh? My dad will never believe it.'

I watched him cross the road and dribble an imaginary ball along the pavement, before thumping it home between two parked cars. He stood with both arms in the air, head thrown back, taking the applause of the crowd on the empty street. Sometimes I seriously worry about Kenny.

Nine into Five

'We're still one player short,' Kenny reminded me as we walked into school on Monday morning. 'Who are we going to ask?'

I'd already given the matter some thought. So far, we'd decided on four players for the Eagles—Martin, Rashid, Kenny, and me. I hadn't asked Martin and Rashid yet but I was pretty sure they'd leap at the chance to play. After all, anyone who turned down a chance of playing at the City ground would need their head examined.

Martin was the obvious choice for goalkeeper. Apart from being the school goalie, he's the best keeper I know. He's not much taller than me but he's fast on his feet and a great shot stopper. Rashid is another of my friends who's in the school team. He plays as a central defender and he's got long legs that he uses to steal the ball away from you just when you think you've got past him. I knew I could rely on Rashid to keep things tight at the back. He didn't go wandering upfield in search of glory like most defenders I know. That left Kenny and me. It would be my job to score the goals and Kenny could—well, Kenny could make a nuisance of himself (probably to both sides).

Martin, Rashid, Kenny, and me—it still left us one player short. I'd run through the team in my head a hundred times and I hadn't yet come up with the fifth player. It wasn't that we were short of choices, I could have asked anyone in the school, but we didn't need just anyone. Whoever we chose had to be good enough to make up for Kenny's shortcomings in midfield. It had to be someone who could tackle hard, run with the ball, and preferably score goals too. (I couldn't do it all by myself.)

As Kenny and I walked into the playground a football hummed through the air, narrowly missing my head. It thumped against the railings and rebounded at my feet.

'Hey, careful!' I said. 'That nearly—'

I stopped in mid sentence. The boy coming to retrieve the ball was Steve Spicer. He eyed me from under his dark fringe of hair.

'Yeah?'

'Nothing,' I said. 'Sorry, I . . . I wasn't looking, Steve.'

Spicer nodded. He flicked the ball up with his foot and caught it neatly. Then he ran back to the game he was playing.

'Sorry, Steve,' mimicked Kenny in a grovelling voice. 'Sorry, did my head get in the way of your ball, Steve?'

I wasn't listening. I was staring after the fifth player we needed for Endsley Eagles. It was amazing that I'd never thought of it before.

'Spicer?' Kenny was incredulous. 'You've got to be joking!'

'Why?' I said. 'He's the best player in the school.'

'Yes, but you know what he's like,' argued Kenny. 'He's a psycho. He should be locked up.'

'Yes,' I agreed. 'But he's also a fantastic footballer.'

'And he's a big head,' Kenny went on. 'He thinks he can boss everyone around.'

'I'm not asking you to like him,' I said. 'We just get him to help us win the tournament.'

'No,' said Kenny flatly. 'He'll spoil everything. Anyway, there are loads of other people we could ask.'

We were interrupted by the bell calling us into school so we didn't finish the argument. Yet the more I thought about it, the more the idea grew on me. Spicer was exactly what we needed.

I was once substitute for a school match where the opposing team had a slight, fair-haired lad who was a good dribbler. His favourite trick was to roll the ball under his foot and dart away before you could tackle him. He tried this trick successfully three or four times in the opening ten minutes of the game. Then he came face to face with Spicer. The two of them stood facing each other—the fair-haired lad with his foot on the ball, Spicer watching him like a wolf eyeing his dinner. The lad rolled the ball under his foot. A second later he was catapulted into the air as Spicer bowled him over with the force of a hurricane and steamed away with the ball. The referee awarded a foul but Spicer had made his point. After that the tricky dribbler hung out on the wing and passed the ball whenever it came his way.

Spicer played football as if he was waging a personal war. There was a furious energy about him. I'd seen him ride three or four tackles on his way into the penalty area, brushing defenders aside like fleas, before thumping the ball venomously into the net. Everyone in our school was scared of him and with good reason. Spicer had a reputation for getting into fights and no one in their right mind wanted to fight him.

Needless to say, Spicer wasn't a friend of ours. Kenny and I instinctively kept well out of his way, which was easy since he wasn't in our class. Yet the more I considered it, the more I thought it made perfect sense. Spicer was the key to us winning the tournament. With him on our side we'd be unbeatable and Robbie Kidd's autograph would be mine for the asking. There was only one question—could I persuade Spicer to play for us?

At break time I spoke to Martin and Rashid who, as I predicted, both eagerly accepted the invitation to play for the Eagles. The prospect of playing at the City ground was enough to make them bug-eyed with excitement.

Martin decided the tournament was just a way of talent spotting youngsters to play for City. 'You wait,' he assured us. 'If we reach the final, they'll sign me up afterwards. There'll be dozens of talent scouts watching, that's the whole point.'

When I mentioned Spicer might be playing for us, they were both astounded.

'Really?' said Rashid. 'How did you get him?'

'Well, I haven't yet,' I said casually. 'But he's bound to say yes. I'm going to have a chat with him later.' Martin and Rashid exchanged looks. 'Having a chat' with Spicer was like saying you were going swimming with sharks.

As it turned out I had the chance to speak to Spicer at lunch time. I spotted him sitting on a table next to Todd Morton, eating his lunch. Todd Morton was a red-haired, freckly boy who played up front for the school team. He hung around Spicer like a pet puppy, wagging his tail whenever Spicer gave him an order.

I approached the table rather nervously, carrying my tray. I still hadn't worked out how I was going to start the conversation.

'Hi,' I said. 'Anyone sitting here?' I indicated the chair opposite Spicer with a nod.

Spicer looked at the empty chair, then at me. 'You trying to be funny?'

'No, no,' I said quickly. 'I just wondered if maybe someone was sitting here and you were saving it for them till they got back—or something.'

I was starting to babble so I sat down quickly and busied myself eating my beefburger and chips. Spicer and Todd Morton carried on finishing their apple crumble as if I wasn't there. Neither of them spoke. Spicer was hunched over his bowl with his arms round it, as if someone might try to steal it from him. (Rumour had it there were three older Spicer brothers at home, each bigger and meaner than he was.) He ate quickly, spooning the pudding into his mouth and slurping noisily. There was a small piece of crumble stuck to his cheek. Before I'd worked out how to open the conversation, he slid his empty bowl across to Todd.

'Right, I'm off. Take that to the hatch for me.' He stood up and pushed his chair back.

Sensing it was now or never, I took a breath. 'Wait,' I said. 'Steve, there's something I wanted to ask you.'

Spicer looked at me as if he'd forgotten I was there. 'Yeah?'

'It's just I'm getting this team together for a tournament.'

'What sort of team? Tiddlywinks?' said Spicer. He glanced at Todd Morton who sniggered on cue.

'A football team,' I said. 'Five-a-side. We're called Endsley Eagles.'

'Big thrills. So what?'

'Well, so I thought maybe you could play for us. I mean you're the best player in the school so . . .'

Spicer interrupted. 'Why should I play for your crummy little team?'

I paused before playing my ace. 'No reason.

It's just the tournament's being held at the City ground. In fact, the trophy's going to be presented by Robbie Kidd.'

'Robbie Kidd?'

Spicer's mouth had dropped open. Suddenly he was sitting down opposite me paying full attention. Todd Morton had sat down too and they were firing questions at me. When is it? they wanted to know. How did I hear about it? Was I absolutely certain that Robbie Kidd was going to be there? I filled them in on all the details.

'Who else is in the team?' asked Spicer when I'd finished.

'Well, obviously we'll have Martin in goal. Then there's Rashid, me, you, and um . . . Kenny.'

'Kenny? Kenny Bird?' said Spicer. 'That gormless idiot? He can't play to save his life.'

'I know he's not in the school team,' I said. 'But he's not that bad.'

'What about me?' Todd Morton suggested. 'I don't mind playing.'

'Yeah, but we've already got a team,' I said.

Spicer shook his head. 'Todd's ten times better than Birdbrain. You want to win this thing, don't you?'

'Yeah,' I said, 'but we already . . . '

'Anyway you need six,' Spicer interrupted.

'Six?'

'Yeah. You can't enter a tournament without a sub. So with me and Todd that makes six. What's your problem?'

Spicer shook his dark fringe out of his eyes and stared me out. He had an unnerving way of holding your gaze and saying nothing, daring you to disagree with him.

'Nothing,' I said after a pause. 'No problem at all. That's settled then. You and Todd, great.'

Getting up from the table, I walked away. It hadn't gone quite the way I'd planned. Todd Morton was a creep and I hadn't bargained on having him in the team. All the same, he was a decent footballer and the main thing was I'd persuaded Spicer to play. With him on our side, I felt we had a real chance of winning the tournament. All in all I reckoned I'd handled the whole thing pretty well. Spicer hadn't even tried to hit me.

I went out to the playground to look for Kenny and the others to tell them the news. But before I could find them I was stopped by two boys from our class—Andy Smart and Ryan James.

'Is it true?' Andy wanted to know.

'Is what true?' I said.

'That you've got a team and you're going to play at the City ground?'

'Who told you that?' I asked.

'Kenny. He's going round telling everyone he's going to meet Robbie Kidd.'

I rolled my eyes. Trust Kenny to have blabbed it all round the school.

'Yes,' I said. 'It's true, what about it?'

'Let me play,' pleaded Andy. 'I could play up front, you've seen me. Or defence even. I don't mind. I'll play anywhere.'

'The thing is . . . ' I began.

Ryan James cut in. 'What about me? I'm miles better than Kenny. He's useless.'

They both started talking at once, telling me why I'd be mad not to pick them. I found myself backing away until I was pressed up against a wall.

'Look!' I said, finally getting a word in edgeways. 'The thing is, I can't pick either of you. We've got all the players we need.'

'That's not what Kenny told us,' replied Andy. 'He said you were still one player short.'

He took something out of his school bag and placed it in my hands. It was his Premiership Sticker Book which I vaguely remembered admiring at his house once. My own sticker collection had been abandoned after a week but Andy had diligently collected and swapped until he had every player in the Premiership.

'What's this?' I asked.

'It's yours. You can keep it,' said Andy.

'Don't be daft. It took you ages to collect all these.'

'Just think about it,' said Andy. 'That's all I'm saying. I'd give anything to play at the City ground. Anything.'

I sighed heavily. 'Look, I can't promise anything . . . '

Andy grinned and slapped me on the back. 'Thanks, Mark. You won't regret it.'

'And me too?' said Ryan. 'I'm miles better than Kenny. You know I am.'

Before I could say any more they'd walked off, both convinced they were a certainty for the team.

I told you before I can be stupid. My trouble is I just can't say no to people. It's when they look at me in that pleading way. Maybe it's because I know what it feels like not to be picked. It's happened to me loads of times for the school team and it's the worst feeling in the world. So when someone asks me—begs me—to let them play, I say nothing. The problem is nothing turns out to be worse than saying no.

By the end of that day I counted up the players I had for Endsley Eagles. Besides me and Kenny there was now Martin, Rashid, Spicer, Todd, Andy, Ryan, and Danny Lawrence. (I haven't mentioned Danny, he followed me around the rest of that day nagging until I finally gave in and promised to give him a chance.) At the start of the day we were a player short, now we had a squad of nine players, all convinced they were in the team. Don't ask me how it happened. Personally I blamed Kenny for opening his big mouth.

On Trial

It was bound to end in disaster. For the next couple of days I went around hoping the whole mess would sort itself out. Maybe some of the team would get cold feet or go down with chickenpox and I'd miraculously find myself back with only five players again. Of course it didn't happen. With the tournament less than a week away, everyone kept telling me how much they were looking forward to playing.

It was Kenny who suggested the training session. After all, he pointed out, we hadn't got much time to get used to playing together as a team. Rashid and Martin were all in favour and in the end I had to agree. We fixed our first training session to be held in the local park after school on Wednesday. When I mentioned that I'd tell Spicer, Kenny gave me a surprised look.

'Spicer? What for? I thought we weren't asking him.'

'No,' I said. 'You didn't want to ask him, Kenny. I did.'

'Well what about Andy? Didn't you speak to him?'

'Andy . . . ?'

'Yes, you promised he'd be in the team. That's what he told me.'

'I didn't promise anyone!' I said, starting to getting flustered.

'Then who is playing, Mark?' asked Rashid.

'Yeah, who's in the team besides us four?' demanded Martin.

'I . . . um . . . let's just see who turns up,' I said and walked away quickly, before they could ask any more questions.

Word about the training session soon got around. The news that Endsley Eagles were going to play in a tournament at the City ground had become the talk of the school. People in my class were treating me with a new

respect and I noticed younger kids pointing me out in the playground to their friends. 'That's Mark Denton. The one who's going to meet Robbie Kidd and get his autograph.' (Kenny had told everyone about my quest to get the last autograph.) I would have enjoyed the attention, if I hadn't been so worried about the training session. The questions kept buzzing round my head. Who was I going to leave out? And, worse still, how was I going to break it to them? If I told Andy, Ryan, or Danny they were out, they'd accuse me of breaking promises. If I dropped Spicer or Todd I might as well dig my own grave and jump in to save them the trouble of killing me. The way I saw it, at least four people were going to end up hating me by the end of the day. I was beginning to wish I'd never started to manage my own football team.

I was late getting to the park, because for a long time I'd sat in my bedroom looking at my autograph book. I stared at the blank page in the book—the one waiting for Robbie Kidd's signature. This was the reason I'd started the Eagles, I reminded myself. The whole point of entering the tournament was to win. If we were knocked out before the final there was no certainty I'd get close enough to Robbie Kidd to ask for his autograph. Managers can't afford to be popular, I thought. You just have to pick your best side and it's tough on whoever is left out.

I arrived at the park resolved that I was going to make some hard decisions. But my heart sank when I saw the others waiting for me by the pitch. They were all there—all nine of them—and the arguments had started already.

Spicer turned on me before I'd even had a chance to say hello.

'What's going on? Who invited this bunch of losers?' he demanded.

'Tell him, Mark,' complained Andy. 'Tell Spicer I'm in the team.'

'Yes, and tell him he can go home and take Freckles with him too,' said Kenny, pointing at Todd.

'Watch it, Birdbrain,' said Spicer, taking a step forward.

Things were getting out of hand. Luckily Rashid stepped between Kenny and Spicer, trying to calm everyone down.

'It's your team, Mark,' he said. 'Just tell us who's playing. Then we can get started.'

Everyone looked at me. And that's when the solution came to me out of the blue. I didn't know why I'd never thought of it before. Nine players was almost enough for *two* five-a-side teams.

'I can explain,' I said. 'We're going to have a trial game.'

'A what?' asked Kenny.

'A trial game. You know, just like a professional club. They watch you play in a match and then they pick the best players from either side.'

'Hang on,' said Kenny. 'I thought this was a training session. We already picked the team, Mark. We agreed on it.' A note of panic was creeping into his voice which I tried to ignore.

'What's up, Speccy?' taunted Spicer. 'Scared you're not good enough?'

'Suits me,' said Todd Morton with a shrug. 'I'll play against anyone.'

Danny Lawrence nodded. 'Why not? A trial's fair to everyone. As long as there's no favouritism, Mark.'

I promised I would be impartial. Only Kenny looked unhappy with the idea. I avoided his gaze as we picked sides with Spicer and myself as captains. I picked Martin, Rashid, Ryan, and Kenny on my side. Spicer picked Todd, Andy, and Danny. The sides weren't even but that didn't seem to bother Spicer unduly. He probably felt he was worth two of us in any case.

We lined up for kick off with Martin in goal, Rashid and Ryan in defence, and Kenny and me up front. 'Pass it around and keep it away from Spicer,' I whispered to Kenny.

Kenny didn't answer, evidently still sulking that he had to go through with this charade. He pushed his glasses up his nose and squared his bony shoulders. As usual he was wearing his one and only football shirt, an old City one that had been washed so many times the blue had faded to a dirty grey.

From kick-off I passed the ball to Kenny who knocked it back to Rashid. Rashid brought the ball forward and slipped it out to me on the wing. Andy slid in to tackle me but I side-stepped him and spotted Kenny in space near the goal. 'Kenny!' I shouted and sent him a perfect pass. Normally I would have tried to score myself, but I was still feeling guilty. I wanted to give Kenny every chance to prove he was worth his place in the team.

Kenny collected the ball with his back to goal and turned to try and shoot. Unfortunately he'd forgotten completely about Spicer. At the last moment, he tried to jump out of the way, but it was too late. The crunch of the tackle could be heard all over the park.

'Yeeearggh!' howled Kenny and collapsed to the ground, holding his leg.

Spicer moved away with the ball, without even a backward glance. In a few strides he was past me and bearing down on our goal. To his credit,

Rashid tried to tackle him, but Spicer surged past him as if he wasn't there. He struck his shot hard and low towards the corner. It looked like a certain goal until Martin dived full length and got his fingertips to it, turning it round the pile of coats we were using for goal posts.

'Great save, Martin!' I shouted. Spicer shook his head, furious with himself for not scoring. He collected the ball to take the corner himself while I ran back to help Rashid and Ryan defend. Looking upfield, I could see Kenny still limping around, rubbing his leg and looking aggrieved. Spicer hit an inswinging corner aimed towards the near post. I stepped forward to head it away but Todd Morton suddenly appeared in front of me and glanced the ball into the empty goal.

'We practised that one for the school team,' he gloated. 'Works every time.'

'Come on, Kenny,' I said under my breath as we lined up to take the kick off. 'They're making us look stupid.'

Kenny was still seething about Spicer's tackle on him. 'He's an animal,' he muttered. 'They should put him in the zoo.'

Things didn't get any better. The game continued to be one-way traffic, even though we were the side with the extra player. In our defence Ryan was scared stiff of Spicer, which left Rashid to try and hold out on his own. Time and again, Martin had to pull off a great save to keep us in the game. Even so, it wasn't long before the score crept up to 5–0. Todd scored twice while Spicer helped himself to a hat trick. I managed to pull one goal back with a long shot that Danny fumbled in goal, but that was the only reply we managed.

Kenny had been little more than a spectator since Spicer had flattened him. He limped around upfield and occasionally called for a pass without much conviction. Then, right near the end of the game, he was gifted the best chance of the game. Rashid broke up an attack and swept the ball upfield to find Kenny unmarked and with a clear run on goal. By the time Spicer was hot on his heels, Kenny was into the penalty area and looked certain to score.

'Shoot, Kenny! Shoot!' I shouted, seeing Spicer gathering himself for a sliding tackle.

Maybe it was the fear of another one of Spicer's crunching tackles that put him off. Or maybe it was knowing that everyone expected him to score. Whatever the reason, the pressure was too much. Kenny sliced the ball off the outside of his boot and watched it miss the goal by a mile. The ball struck a low branch of a tree and sent a flock of startled sparrows twittering into the sky.

Some of the others hooted with laughter. 'Nice shooting, Birdbrain!' said Spicer, patting Kenny on the head.

I called a halt to the game soon after that. I'd seen more than enough.

The others gathered round me, panting to catch their breath.

'Well?' said Spicer. 'Let's hear it then, captain. Tell us the team.'

Fall Out

They were all looking at me expectantly and I knew the decision couldn't be put off any longer. It was better to get it over with.

'OK,' I said, trying not to look anyone in the eye. 'I can't pick everyone, so here it is. In goal Martin. Rashid in defence. Midfield— me and Steve,' I said, nodding at Spicer. 'Up front . . . ' I paused. 'Up front we'll play Todd.'

There was a groan from Andy, Ryan, and Danny. They shook their heads in disbelief. That didn't bother me so much as Kenny. He was standing pale and tight-lipped at the back of the group. He hadn't spoken a word but he was staring at me resentfully.

'Kenny, I'd like you to be sub . . . ' I began.

'You can stick it,' he said, his voice thick and harsh.

'Come on, Kenny . . . '

'No! Stuff that!' He was shaking with anger now. 'I don't want to be sub for your poxy team, Mark.'

He turned to walk away, but swung round again after only a few steps.

'You want to know something?' he said. 'There wouldn't be an Endsley Eagles if it wasn't for me. I was the one who saw the report in the paper. I helped to think of the name. It was us who started this team, Mark, remember? You and me. And now you've got the nerve to say I can be sub, like you're doing me a big favour. Well, thanks, thanks a lot, but you can stick it.'

Kenny stalked off towards the park gate, his socks rolled down to his pale thin ankles. I had a strong urge to run after him and grab him by the arm. To say it was all a joke, that he was right, that the Eagles were as much his team as mine, but it was way too late for that.

Spicer watched him go with a thin smile. 'Ahh, poor baby,' he said. 'Let him go crying to his mum.'

The next morning, Kenny didn't call for me on the way to school. Most days he drops in about quarter to nine and we walk the last part of the journey together. But on Thursday I waited until ten to nine and there was no ring at the door bell.

I didn't blame him for still being mad at me. I knew how much it meant to him playing at the City ground. He'd told everyone at school about it, and now the word would go round that he'd been dropped from the team. It was humiliating and it was all my fault. But, put yourself in my shoes, what else could I have done? How could I pick Kenny after the way he played in that trial game? It would have been obvious to everyone that I was just choosing my best friend. Even Kenny's own mother wouldn't have picked him after that open goal he missed. I had to leave him out to be fair to

43

the others. And besides, there was another reason—I wanted to win the tournament and I wanted Robbie Kidd's autograph. If I was honest it was a relief that I had an excuse to drop Kenny.

All the same, don't get the idea I felt good about it. And I didn't feel any better when I got to school. There was Kenny standing in the playground with Andy Smart and Ryan James. As I walked by they all turned and looked at me as if I'd crawled out from under a stone.

'Got my sticker book?' demanded Andy.

I pulled it out of my school bag and handed it over. I'd never asked for it in the first place so I didn't know why he was acting all high and mighty.

Kenny didn't say anything, didn't even give a nod in my direction. He went back to telling Andy and Ryan about some goofy programme he'd been watching on TV the night before. I walked off and left the three of them to it. It felt strange standing on my own in the playground, hoping that the bell would go soon.

The rest of the day it was the same story.

Kenny hung around with his new buddies, Andy and Ryan, and avoided me like the plague. He even moved tables in class so that he wouldn't have to sit next to me.

At afternoon break I went looking for Martin and Rashid and caught up with them in the playground.

'It's OK,' said Martin when he saw me. 'We already know.'

'Know what?' I asked mystified.

'About training tonight. Didn't Spicer talk to you about it?'

'No,' I said, 'I haven't seen him all day.'

'Oh.' Martin looked a little uncomfortable.

'Anyway,' said Rashid, 'we're meeting at four at the old scout hut. Spicer reckons we need to practise five-a-side rules and the scout hut's better than the park.'

'The goals are just the right size,' enthused Martin.

'Just hold on,' I said. 'How come no one's asked me about this?'

Neither of them answered.

'I thought I was captain of this team?'

' ''Course you are, Mark,' said Rashid.

'Then how come Spicer is fixing training sessions and telling you all what to do?'

Martin looked at the ground, sullenly. 'It's not our fault. Talk to Spicer,' he said.

I couldn't find Spicer before the end of break and there was no sign of him at the end of school either. I decided the only thing I could do was turn up at the scout hut like everyone else and try to straighten things out with him. I couldn't help feeling annoyed. I was the one who'd invited Spicer to play for the Eagles in the first place and now he was acting as if it was his team. It was stupid, I know, but I even started to wonder if he'd planned to tell me about the training session. It seemed as if Spicer had made sure to inform everyone except me. What was going on?

Votes for Captain

At four o'clock, I made my way along the overgrown path to the meeting place. The old scout hut was a shabby building at the end of Church Road. In fact, it hadn't been used as a scout hut for years but the name had stuck. Nettles grew around the entrance and there was a rusty padlock on the door. In any case we were more interested in what lay round the back. Following the path through a wilderness of trees and bushes, you eventually came to some steps which led down unexpectedly to an ancient tennis court. The net had disappeared long ago, leaving only the faint outline of the court on the cracked surface. It made a perfect five-a-side pitch which someone had recognized by painting the outline of goal posts at either end on the wooden boards that skirted the wire fencing.

As I reached the path, I could hear voices coming from the court at the back. The others had evidently arrived before me. Below me I could hear one voice louder and more insistent than the others. It was unmistakably Spicer's and something made me hang back behind the corner of the scout hut to listen.

'The captain's always the best player,' he was saying. 'You look at any professional team.'

'Yeah, Steve, but it's not your team. It's Mark's. He started it.' The second voice was Rashid's.

'So what?' said Spicer. 'Any idiot can fill in a form. I could have done it.'

'But you didn't. Endsley Eagles was Mark's idea.'

Spicer tried a different tack. 'OK, fine, don't say I didn't warn you. If you want to get knocked out first round it's up to you.'

'You don't think we stand a chance?' asked Martin, worriedly.

'Not with a loser like Mark Denton as captain.'

Another voice joined in, Todd Morton's. 'Steve should be captain. It's obvious. He's worth ten of Denton.'

It was fast dawning on me why Spicer hadn't told me about this 'training session'. With me out of the way he was trying to bully the others into making him captain. I couldn't believe his nerve.

'Tell 'em, Steve,' Todd was saying. 'Tell 'em what we talked about earlier.'

Spicer ignored him. 'The point is, everyone here plays for the school team, right? Me, Todd, Martin, and you Rashid. There's only player who isn't good enough.'

'Mark's played for the school team,' protested Rashid.

'Only when we're desperate,' sneered Spicer. 'He never gets a full game. And he reckons he's a striker but let's face it, when did he last score a goal?'

Nobody answered. It was a sore point with me that I'd never scored for the school team.

It's not easy to score when you're only allowed on as sub for the last ten minutes.

Spicer went on, hammering home his argument. 'Think about it. You'll never get another chance like this. Do you want to lose just because of one player?'

'Steve's right,' bleated Todd.

'Ask yourself why is Denton in the team? I'll tell you. Because he picked it, that's why.'

'He's a passenger,' agreed Todd.

'Wait a minute!' Rashid protested. 'Are you saying we kick Mark out? Out of his own team?'

'It's not his team any more,' said Spicer coolly. 'If I'm captain, I pick the side. And I say he's not good enough.'

Something snapped in me when I heard that. All the time I'd been listening to Spicer I was getting more wound up and now I felt I'd explode if I heard another word. In seconds I was bounding down the steps and on to the court. Every face turned towards me in surprise and, for once, even Spicer looked taken aback. He obviously hadn't expected to see me and now he was wondering how much I'd overheard.

'Mark. We were just waiting for you,' he said, forcing a smile.

'Oh were you?' I said. 'Funny, because from what I just heard, you can't wait to get rid of me.' My heart was thumping in my chest and I was breathing hard.

'We weren't in on this, Mark,' Rashid said quietly. 'This was all Spicer's idea.'

I turned back to Spicer, who stood his ground, glaring defiantly.

'Well, it's true, I should be captain. I'm the only decent player in this crummy team and you know it.'

'Well, besides me,' said Todd.

'Shut up!' ordered Spicer. He took a step

forward so that I could feel his warm breath on my face. 'What are you going to do, Markie boy, fight me for it? Go ahead.'

By now I was so enraged, I was ready to throw myself on top of Spicer and take my chances. All that stopped me was knowing that a fight was exactly what Spicer wanted. If he could reduce it to a slugging contest, I knew there'd be only one winner, and it wouldn't be me. Instead I took a step back. 'OK. Fair's fair. There are five of us here. Let's take a vote on it. Who wants Spicer as captain?'

Todd's hand went up immediately. Spicer raised his own hand in the air and glowered at Martin and Rashid. Martin shifted uneasily, but neither of them made a move.

'Who votes I stay as captain?' I asked. My own hand went up and was joined by Rashid's. For a moment I thought my plan might backfire. Martin was hesitating, caught between loyalty to me and fear of what Spicer might do to him. At last, slowly, he raised his hand in the air.

'That settles it then,' I said. 'Three votes to

two. I'm still captain and since I pick the side, I'm dropping you, Spicer. You're off the team.'

'You what?' croaked Spicer in disbelief.

'You heard. We don't need you. Get lost.'

Spicer gave a hollow laugh. 'You're rubbish without me. I'm the only decent player you've got.'

'Not any more.' I said. 'And you can take your freckle-faced poodle with you. We won't be needing him either.'

Spicer narrowed his eyes and bared his yellow teeth. For a moment I thought he was going to lunge at me and pin me to the ground. Then he turned on his heel and stalked off up the steps, with Todd scampering after him. 'You wait, Denton,' he spat back over his shoulder. 'You'll be sorry for this.'

We waited in silence until he'd disappeared, then Rashid burst out laughing.

'Blimey! You were taking a chance, Mark. I thought he was going to murder you!'

'So did I,' I said. I realized my hands were still shaking and hid them in my pockets. 'Anyway. We're better off without those two creeps.'

'Yeah,' said Martin. 'But before you get too pleased with yourself, aren't you forgetting something?'

'What?'

'How are we going to win the tournament with only three players?'

Kenny

'Oh, it's you,' said Kenny sourly. 'I thought you'd be out training for the big day. If you want me to come and cheer you on, you're wasting your time.'

It was Friday afternoon—just one week before the tournament—and I was standing at Kenny's front door. I came straight to the point.

'We need you back on the team, Kenny.'

'Yeah sure. As sub,' he said.

'No, in the team. Midfield dynamo. What do you say?'

Kenny's eyes lit up for a second. Then he remembered the way I'd treated him and the blank look returned. He wasn't going to let me off the hook that easily.

'What's made you change your mind?' he asked. 'I thought I wasn't good enough for you.'

Briefly I explained to him what had happened last night at the scout hut.

'Huh,' grunted Kenny with satisfaction. 'Told you, didn't I? I told you Spicer would try to take over.'

'I know,' I admitted. 'I should have listened.'

'So the truth is you only want me back because you can't get a team?'

'Come on, Kenny,' I said. 'There are hundreds of other people we could ask.'

'Great. Why don't you then?'

I sighed. This was proving harder than I'd expected. 'Look, I'm sorry, OK, Kenny? I just got carried away with the idea of winning. I made a mistake and I'm sorry. What else do you want me to say?'

Kenny looked away. 'You could say you think I'm good enough.'

So that's what was eating him. 'Kenny,' I said, 'you're worth ten of Spicer any day.'

His face finally broke into a grin. 'Yeah

right,' he said. 'I'll remind you of that next time I miss an open goal.'

'So does that mean you'll play?'

'Are you kidding? Think I'm gonna miss the chance to play at the City ground? Anyway, I want to be there to make sure Robbie Kidd signs your autograph book. Then I won't have to listen to you droning on about it for another year.'

Kenny was off then, talking tactics and outlining how he thought we should approach our first game. I couldn't help smiling as we walked down to the park to meet the others. The great thing about Kenny is he can't hold a grudge for long. I guessed that the past few days had been as much of a torture to him as they were to me. OK, Kenny may not be the greatest footballer in the world, but I realized I felt better having my best friend back on the team. Kenny is a born optimist and there wasn't a flicker of doubt in his mind that we could win the tournament—Spicer or no Spicer.

'After all,' he reasoned. 'It's like the FA Cup. Anything can happen in a knock-out tournament. We've only got to win a few games and suddenly we're in the final.'

In the week that followed we trained harder than we'd ever done in our lives. Andy Smart didn't need much persuasion to rejoin the team and we discovered that when we tried him in defence he was a natural. I couldn't understand why he'd been trying to play as a striker all this time. Andy's built like a miniature tank and he hasn't got the speed to play up front. Put him in defence alongside Rashid, however, and he was as steady as a rock.

There was one thing we still needed—a coach. Over breakfast on Saturday morning I happened to mention to my dad that we were having trouble with our free kick routines. Dad used to be a referee in amateur football and he took the bait, just as I'd hoped. Soon he was down at the park with us every evening, helping us prepare for the tournament. He had us playing two-touch football so that we learned to move the ball quickly from one player to another. We spent hours crossing the ball and shooting first time, aiming low for the corners the way he taught us. Even Kenny started to gain in confidence in front of goal and was less of a danger to passing seagulls.

Finally we worked on a free kick routine where I pretended I was going hit the ball but at the last moment rolled it to one side for Rashid to shoot. Seven or eight times out of ten it worked with the ball ending up in the net, even though Martin in goal knew what was coming.

At last, the night before the tournament, Dad said we were ready. 'It's up to you now,' he told us. 'You've put in all the hard work, now you've got to make it count on the day. There'll be other good teams, but don't worry about them. You just go out and play the way we've been practising.'

Friday night finally arrived and we piled into two cars and drove to the City ground. The sight of the stadium towering over us made my stomach lurch. I'd been to the ground dozens of times before but that was to watch City play. This time it would be us out there on the pitch. The car park was packed with cars and mini-buses, while groups of boys stood around in their kit, shivering in the cold wind.

'Blimey!' I said. 'How many people do you think are here?'

'Probably more than City get for a home game,' laughed my dad. 'At least we might see some decent football tonight.'

'I wonder if that's Robbie Kidd's car,' said Kenny as we parked near a gleaming silver Jaguar. 'I hope you've got your autograph book, Mark.'

For the hundredth time that evening I

checked in the pocket of my sports bag. The autograph book was safe inside. Even if we didn't win the tournament, I tried to tell myself, I'd be happy if I went home with Robbie's signature on the blank page in my book. I wondered if he would be there from the start to watch any of our matches. The thought only made me more nervous. What if we froze when we got out on the pitch and were trounced in the very first round? I tried to put such worries out of my mind, as my dad went in search of a club steward. We were eventually directed towards a large grey building resembling an aircraft hanger. Inside, to our surprise and disappointment, we found ourselves looking at an indoor football pitch.

'Is this where we're playing?' grumbled Kenny. 'I thought we'd be on the actual turf.'

'Don't be daft,' said Rashid. 'They're not going to let a load of kids ruin the pitch, are they?'

'This is better anyway,' said my dad. 'It's a proper five-a-side pitch, you can play the ball off the walls.' He started to point out where we weren't allowed inside the goalkeeper's area but he was interrupted by Kenny.

'Look over there! What's he doing here?'

Standing with a team I'd never seen before was Spicer. He was kitted out like the rest of them in a smart all white strip with a silver star emblazoned on the chest. Our team looked shabby in comparison, in our motley collection of replica City shirts from various seasons. As we were staring, Spicer happened to look our way and came striding over, wearing a smug look on his face.

'So, managed to scrape a team together, did you?'

'Who's that lot you're with?' I asked.

'Astley All Stars,' said Spicer. 'My mate Jason is captain. When they heard I was free, they practically begged me to play for them.'

'That desperate, were they?' said Kenny.

Spicer regarded him icily. 'I hope you're wearing your shin pads, Speccy,' he said. 'You'll need them if I come near you.'

'Well, thanks for coming over,' I said. 'Your mates will be worried about you.'

Spicer gave us a parting smile. 'Try not to get knocked out too early,' he said. 'I'm looking forward to playing you lot.' He jogged back to join his team on the other side of the hall.

Rashid appeared at my shoulder. 'I know that team,' he said. 'I've played against them in the Sunday league.'

'Any good?' I asked.

'Top of the table. It makes you sick, they could probably win this without Spicer.'

I told Rashid it was probably better to keep this information to himself. The rest of our team looked nervous enough without adding to their worries. Kenny was fiddling with his glasses while Andy disappeared to the toilet every five minutes. Neither of them had played in a real match before, let alone in front of a crowd this big. I looked around, hoping to catch a glimpse of Robbie Kidd. There were a number of City's training staff, recognizable by their club tracksuits, but no sign of the star attraction.

The draw for the tournament was displayed on a board behind one goal. There were sixteen teams entered which, according to my calculations meant that we had to win three games if we wanted to reach the final. It didn't sound much—three games, but I had no idea what we were up against. Our first round game was against a team called Cosby Kites. However, when our name was called and we ran out on the pitch, the other team didn't appear. We waited around for five minutes taking practice shots at Martin, but no one could find any trace of the Kites.

'Maybe they've flown off,' suggested Kenny.

Eventually the referee informed us we'd been given a bye into the second round.

'What's a buy?' Andy wanted to know. 'Do we have to pay?'

'No, you big dope,' said Rashid. 'It means we go through.'

'Well, that's great,' said Kenny. 'We're in the second round without having kicked a ball.'

I wasn't so sure. All the waiting around only made me more anxious. Personally I'd rather have got a game under our belts to help settle our nerves. We watched as Spicer's team, the

All Stars, played their first round game and won it without breaking sweat, 5–0.

Andy shook his head when the game was over. 'I hope we don't get drawn against them. It'll be a massacre.'

Finally, our second round match came round, against a team called Parkside Rangers. It took us most of the first half to get into the game. At first we were so nervous, we kept making stupid mistakes and giving the ball away. Then, just before half-time, Rashid took a snap shot from a distance and the goalie almost fumbled it, grabbing it at the second attempt. That gave us confidence and we started to string some passes together. 'Shoot on sight,' I told the others at half-time. 'Aim low for the corners like we practised. The goalie looks dodgy to me.' The plan worked. We won the game 2–1, with goals from Andy and me, though mine was a soft shot the goalkeeper let under his body.

It didn't matter to us, when the whistle went for full-time we were delirious. Kenny went round slapping everyone on the back as if we'd just won the tournament.

'Well done,' my dad said, as we trooped off. 'You can take confidence from that second half. You were starting to play as a team. But they won't all be as easy as that. You've got the semi-final next, so you'll have to improve.'

Again we watched Spicer's All Stars stroll through their match, winning 4–1 with Spicer claiming a hat trick. Mercifully we weren't drawn against them in the semi-final but against a team called Tornadoes. They played in an all red strip and they came on to the pitch like they meant business.

'Look at the size of that number three,' Kenny whispered to me. 'You sure these are all under twelve?'

'Size doesn't mean anything,' I said. 'They're probably all fat and slow.'

The Tornadoes turned out to be far from slow, but they didn't mind using their weight. Several times I was elbowed off the ball by the beefy number three I was up against. At half-time there was nothing between us with the

score at 0–0. Martin had kept us in the game with a great one-handed save while at the other end Kenny had fluffed our only chance.

The second half was much the same, with chances going begging at either end. Then, with a few minutes left, we got a free kick, just outside the goalkeeper's area. It was perfect for what we'd practised in training. The Tornadoes made a three man wall in front of their goal area. I placed the ball and took a long run up as if I was going to try and blast it right through them. At the last moment I checked and rolled the ball to my right where Rashid had ghosted up unnoticed. He struck his shot with the outside of his boot and saw it swerve past the unsighted goalkeeper and into the net.

One–nil. The whistle went soon afterwards and I almost collapsed with relief and exhaustion.

'Well done, lads! Brilliant!' said my dad, putting his arm round me.

'We did it!' Kenny shouted. 'I can't believe it. We did it! We're in the final.'

'Yeah,' said Rashid. 'And guess who we'll be playing.'

He was pointing behind us. We turned to see Steve Spicer gloating across at us. Astley All Stars had still to play their semi-final, but it would take a miracle to stop them reaching the final. That meant if we wanted to win the trophy we'd have to beat

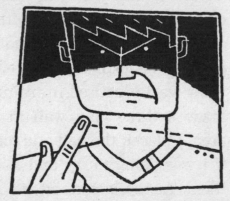

them. Spicer mouthed something that I couldn't make out, then drew a finger across his throat in a gesture we all understood. They were going to murder us.

Final Chance

'Listen,' I said. 'We've got this far. What's to stop us going out and winning this?'

'Are you blind?' said Andy. 'You saw them, Mark. We'll get creamed.'

'Not if we play like we did in the semi,' I argued.

'Let's just try and keep the score down,' said Martin dejectedly. 'I don't want to be picking the ball out of the net six or seven times.'

I shook my head in exasperation. 'You're all talking as if we've lost before we've started. You didn't think we'd get to the final, but we did it. Why can't we win one more game?'

'Because we're playing Astley All Stars,' answered Rashid gloomily.

Before I could reply, Kenny interrupted. 'Listen to yourselves!' he said, angrily. 'It's only Spicer and his smarmy mates we're playing, not Real Madrid!'

'Come on, Kenny, he's the best player in the school,' said Martin.

Kenny rounded on him. 'So what? Why are you all scared of him? He thinks we're just a bunch of losers. Well, let's go out there and show him. Let's wipe that grin off his big ugly face.'

It wasn't the best team talk I'd ever heard but it struck a nerve. We all hated Spicer. We hadn't forgotten the way he'd tried to bully us into making him captain. Nothing could be more satisfying than beating him in the final. And in any case, what had we got to lose by trying? At least we'd have the satisfaction of showing Spicer we could put up a fight.

Out of the corner of my eye I could see the referee checking his watch. I began to talk fast.

'This is how we're going to play it,' I said. 'I'm going to drop back to help Rashid and Andy. We'll have a three man defence and we won't let them past. If one of us gets beaten someone else gets back to cover, right?'

'But who's playing striker?' said Andy.

I turned to Kenny. 'That'll be up to you,' I said. 'Chase everything and don't give them any time on the ball. We've got to frustrate them, put them off their game. Then we hit them on the counter attack and Kenny grabs the winner with one of his thunderbolts.'

Everyone laughed. It was hard to imagine a Kenny thunderbolt. So far the only shot he'd managed was so feeble the goalkeeper could have kept it out with a feather duster.

We ran out on to the pitch for the final. Looking over to the presentation table I saw a figure in a leather jacket emerge through the crowd and shake hands with someone. Robbie

Kidd had arrived just in time for the final. Trust him, I thought, to make his entrance at the last minute. There wasn't time for me to go over and ask for his autograph now. Besides I was too keyed up for the final. I'd have to wait until after the game and hope that the runners up would also be presented with medals. Despite what I'd said to the others I thought the best we could hope for was to keep the scoreline respectable.

As captain I went forward for the toss of the coin to choose ends. The All Stars captain was Spicer's friend Jason. He paused to juggle a ball on his knee and volley it off the pitch. Then he grinned at me, revealing a mouthful of fillings. 'Steve says you lot are so rubbish he walked out on you.'

'Yeah?' I replied. 'Well, he would say that. Nobody likes being dropped, do they?'

Jason's smile faded rapidly; he couldn't tell whether I was joking or not. Round one to the Eagles, I thought, and followed up by winning the toss.

That looked like the only thing we would win. From the kick off the All Stars poured forward and laid siege to our goal. In the first minute Martin had to beat out a stinging shot with his hands, just managing to grab the ball before it bounced out of the area where white shirts were waiting ready to pounce.

'Don't give them space to shoot,' I urged the others. 'Close them down quickly.'

Rashid, Andy, and I spread ourselves in a cordon in front of our goal area. The All Stars seemed puzzled by our reluctance to come out of our own half and attack them. Kenny meanwhile chased the ball from one white shirt to the next like an excited terrier.

'Somebody get rid of this nut,' complained Jason. 'He's making me dizzy.'

Gradually our tactics began to work and impatience crept into the opposition's game. Although they had most of the ball, the All Stars were finding it hard to pierce our three man defence. Rashid in particular was timing his tackles beautifully and bringing the ball away with his long easy stride.

Inevitably it was Spicer who decided enough was enough. As I tried to tackle him,

he pushed the ball past me and sent me sprawling with a shove in the back. Rashid came over to cover but not in time, as Spicer unleashed an unstoppable shot that flew past Martin and crashed against the cross bar making the whole goal shudder. Martin grabbed the ball as it bounced out, but too late, the referee had signalled the ball had crossed the line. Spicer turned away with a look of grim satisfaction and jogged back to the halfway line.

We were grateful to hear the half-time whistle with the score at 1–0.

As we trooped off with our heads down, Spicer brushed past me. 'You wait,' he said.

'We're going to bury you second half. Watch me show you how it's done.'

We stood in a semi-circle, hands on hips and breathing hard.

'It was never over the line,' Martin moaned. 'I saved it. The referee needs Kenny's glasses.'

'Typical,' said Rashid bitterly. 'Just when we were holding out really well.'

'It's not over yet,' I urged. 'All we need is one goal and we're back in it. We'll just have to take a few risks and try to go on the attack.'

As the second half started the All Stars drove forward again, confident that the game was there for the taking. It was just a matter of how many goals they were going to score. Rashid, Andy, and I were forced to defend desperately. But now I started to notice the white shirts weren't passing the ball so smoothly. They were so eager to get their names on the score sheet that they got selfish and held on to the ball too long. This made it easier for us to break up their attacks and it wasn't long before we launched one of our own. With the All Stars backtracking furiously Rashid put me through with only Jason barring my way on the edge of the goalkeeper's area. As he advanced, I prodded the ball through his long legs. I knew I'd pushed it too far into the area, but Jason wasn't taking any chances. Before he could stop himself he'd snaked out a leg to slide the ball back to his keeper. The referee blew a shrill blast on his whistle and pointed to the spot.

'Penalty,' he said. 'The ball was inside the area.'

'Yesss!' I shouted, punching the air. But my joy was cut short when I realized we hadn't chosen anyone to take penalties.

'You take it,' I said to Rashid. 'You're good under pressure.'

'No fear,' said Rashid. 'You take it, you're the captain.'

No one else in the team wanted the responsibility. As I placed the ball on the spot, I couldn't help looking over towards the trophy table. Robbie Kidd was watching me, leaning forward on the barrier so as not to miss anything.

Robbie Kidd is watching me take a penalty! I thought to myself. It was like a dream or maybe a nightmare, I couldn't decide which. I'd seen Robbie take penalties for City. He always tucked them away in the bottom corner, making it look impossibly easy.

'Just imagine you're him,' I told myself. 'Hard and low. Bottom corner. You can do this.'

I took a deep breath, ran up, and struck the ball low to the keeper's right. He guessed correctly and dived full length, one arm outstretched. For an agonizing second I thought he was going to push the ball away but then the net shivered and I realized the ball was in. I'd done it! We'd equalized.

And now the amazing thing happened. All round the arena there was the deafening sound of applause and cheering. Maybe two hundred people or more had stayed to watch the final and it dawned on me that nearly all of them were rooting for us. We were the underdogs and everyone wanted to see us beat the swaggering All Stars. Even Robbie Kidd was grinning and clapping his hands. 1–1 with five minutes to go and now our opponents realized that they had a game on their hands.

As we lined up for kick-off I could see a new determination on the faces of my team mates. The goal had lifted us and with the crowd right behind us, we suddenly felt we might have a chance. However the same thought had obviously occurred to our opponents and they pressed forward, eager to re-establish their superiority. Several times Rashid or I had to make a last ditch tackle to prevent the winning goal. With two minutes left Jason got past me and blasted a shot from the edge of the area. It was moving so fast I was sure Martin was beaten until he flung himself down to his right and somehow came up with the ball in his hands. With the white shirts all committed to attack, Martin bowled the ball upfield and found Kenny on his own, near the halfway line.

'Go, Kenny!' I shouted. 'Take it on your own!'

With a look of blind panic, Kenny turned and set off dribbling towards the other end. Someone flashed past me and I realized with a sinking heart who it was. Spicer was lightning fast and he was already homing in on Kenny like a guided missile.

I was too far behind to help Kenny, I could only watch and pray that he'd have the sense to shoot before it was too late. If felt as if the whole crowd was holding its breath, watching the gap close between the dark shadow of Spicer and the ungainly kid with the specs. Inevitably Kenny looked back at the last minute and saw him coming. I knew what came next, I'd seen this moment before: Kenny would blaze the ball high and wide into the crowd and hang his head in despair. But, just as he drew his foot back to shoot, Spicer lunged across him in a desperate tackle. What happened next seemed to take place in slow motion. I saw the goalkeeper dive to his left to stop Kenny's shot. But instead the ball ricocheted off Spicer's foot and looped high in the air. With the keeper struggling to change direction, the ball floated in a gentle arc dropping down under the bar to nestle in the back of the net.

The crowd erupted in wild cheering. We all ran and mobbed Kenny who was standing, open mouthed, doing a passable impression of a goldfish.

'You did it, Kenny!' I shouted above the noise. 'You scored!'

'Yeah I did,' he said proudly, readjusting his glasses. 'Did you see how I sent the keeper the wrong way?'

Spicer was still slumped on the ground, his head in his hands. He was surrounded by team-mates who were blaming him for putting through his own goal. I couldn't resist patting him on the shoulder as I went past. 'Nice one, Spicer,' I said. 'You really showed us how it's done.'

There was only a minute for us to play out before the referee blew the full time whistle. The All Stars shook their heads in disbelief. They'd been beaten by two goals in the last five minutes when they'd expected to win by a rugby score. Meanwhile we stood on the pitch drinking in the applause, hardly able to believe that we'd won the final.

All too quickly it was time for the presentation and the moment I'd imagined for so long. In a dream I approached the table where Robbie Kidd stood, waiting to hand me the silver trophy, hung with ribbons in City's blue colours.

'Go on, captain,' murmured Kenny behind me. 'This is what you've been waiting for. Ask him for the autograph.'

And that's when I realized that in all the euphoria of winning the game and doing a lap of honour, I'd forgotten the most important thing I had to do.

'I haven't got it,' I said hoarsely.

'What do you mean?' asked Kenny.

'My autograph book. I left it in the pocket of my bag.'

'You big idiot! Run back and get it.'

There wasn't time. I looked for my dad in the crowd and tried to signal frantically to him to bring my bag. He didn't understand and only grinned like a madman, giving me a big thumbs up sign. And, before I could do anything else, we were being ushered forward for the presentation. Robbie Kidd loomed into view and I felt his large, warm hand shaking mine.

'Well done, lads,' he said. 'That was a great come-back.'

I opened my mouth to say something but no words came out. I seemed to have frozen. The next moment a large silver cup was thrust into my hands and somebody had hung a medal round my neck. It should have been the proudest moment of my life, but all I could think was: *I didn't get his autograph. We came*

*all this way and won the cup and I didn't even
ask him. How stupid can you get?*

I moved forward to let Kenny get his medal
and that's when I heard Robbie Kidd say, 'I *knew*
I'd seen you two before. In the hairdresser's,
right? The boy with the nits.'

Turning round I saw Robbie was shaking
Kenny's hand and laughing.

Kenny had turned crimson. 'I haven't
actually got nits,' he muttered. 'Mark made that

up. You see I had to run out because I couldn't afford the haircut.'

'I'm not surprised,' said Robbie Kidd. 'Twenty quid is daylight robbery.' The whole presentation ceremony had come to a standstill while he stood there chatting to the two of us. 'So if you didn't want a hair cut, what were you doing in a hairdresser's?' he asked.

Kenny looked at me. 'Tell him, Mark.'

'I just wanted your autograph,' I said. 'I've been trying to get it for ages. You see I've got this autograph book and I've got everyone else's but not yours. In fact, that's the whole reason we entered this tournament.'

Robbie Kidd looked at me as if it was the best joke he'd ever heard.

'So where is this famous autograph book then?' he laughed.

'It's in my bag over there. Shall I go and get it?'

'Don't worry,' said Robbie. 'I've got a better idea.'

Still smiling to himself, he took out something from his pocket and signed it with a pen. Then he thrust the folded piece of paper into my hand.

'There you are. Don't lose it. You earned that.'

I walked off in a daze, clutching the silver cup in one hand and Robbie Kidd's autograph in the other.

'Well?' said Kenny. 'You finally got it. Let's have a look then.'

I showed him the piece of paper. When I unfolded it I couldn't believe my eyes. Instead of an ordinary piece of paper, Robbie had given me a twenty pound note! Written clearly in blue ink above the queen's head it said:

'To the lads from Robbie Kidd.
Get yourself a haircut!'

'Flippin' Nora!' said Kenny. 'Twenty pounds!'

I gave him a sharp look. 'Don't even think about it,' I said.

Other Oxford books

The Worst Team in the World
Alan MacDonald
ISBN 0 19 275227 8

Reject Rovers are about to make history and get their name in the record books. But it's not the kind of fame they want. If they lose one more game they will officially become the Worst Team of All Time. Something has to be done. But can Kevin 'Panic' Taylor transform his team of no-hopers before Saturday's match?

Nice One, Sam!
John Goodwin
ISBN 0 19 275182 4

Sam is desperate to play up front in his school's next cup match. But he's a hopeless striker.

Then Sam gets IT. The sticker everybody wants and nobody has—Mika Tailer. The best goalie in the world, and Sam's hero. And the sticker changes *everything* . . .

Ryan's United
Dennis Hamley
ISBN 0 19 275120 4

Sometimes life sucks.

I'm a good football player, no, make that a *great* football player, but does anyone appreciate my talents? No.

All I've ever wanted was to have a settled home, with foster parents who cared about me, and, of course, to play football. But every time I think my dream's about to come true, life decides to knock me down and kick me in the guts again!

Maybe one day things will start to go my way for a change, and I'll be part of a winning team . . .

There's Only One Danny Ogle
Helena Pielichaty
ISBN 0 19 275235 9

My name is Danny Ogle and my life is over. Want to know why? We've moved to the countryside—**b-o-r-i-n-g**.

I have to start a new school next week, which I know is going to be terrible. The only good thing is that the school sounds so small they'll be desperate for football players—which means I might, finally, at long last, get into the school team . . .

The Multi-Million Pound Mascot
Chris Powling
ISBN 0 19 275119 0

Josh can't believe it! Of all the people who could have swallowed the Peanut of Power, it had to be his twin sister, Mo. It just isn't fair. She can make all the difference to Oldcastle Athletic's fortunes, but Mo doesn't even like football. She only comes to the match every week for something to do.

The Peanut of Power makes Mo the luckiest girl alive. The trouble is, someone else wants a bit of that luck too—Foxy Freddy, the slimy manager of Oldcastle Athletic. Can he persuade Mo to be the team's lucky mascot?